Is that what friends do?

D1578503

Is that what friends do?

To Amber - M.N.
To Nicola, my best friend - P.B.

A Red Fox Book

Published by Random House Children's Books
20 Vauxhall Bridge Road, London SW1V 2SA

A division of The Random House Group Ltd
London Melbourne Sydney Auckland
Johannesburg and agencies throughout the world

Copyright © Marjorie Newman 1998
Illustrations copyright © Peter Bowman 1998

First published in Great Britain by Hutchinson Children's Books 1998
This Red Fox edition 2000

This book is published subject to the condition that it shall not, by way of trade or otherwise, be lent, resold, hired out,
or otherwise circulated without the publisher's prior consent in any form of binding or cover other than that in which it is
published and without a similar condition including this condition being imposed on the subsequent purchaser.

The rights of Marjorie Newman and Peter Bowman to be identified as the author and illustrator of this work have been
asserted by them in accordance with the Copyright, Designs and Patents Act, 1988.

Printed in China

THE RANDOM HOUSE GROUP Ltd Reg. No. 954009
www.randomhouse.co.uk

ISBN 978 1 849 41443 2

Is that what friends do?

MARJORIE NEWMAN
ILLUSTRATED BY PETER BOWMAN

RED FOX

Elephant sat gloomily on the river bank.
  Monkey came dancing along.
  'Hello, Elephant!' cried Monkey. 'All alone?'
  'Yes,' sighed Elephant.

'So am I!' said Monkey. 'Let's be friends!'

'I've never had a friend before,' said Elephant.
    'I have. Lots!' cried Monkey. 'Why don't you come and stay with me?'

'Is that what friends do?'
asked Elephant.

'Of course!' cried Monkey.

Monkey's doorway was too small for Elephant.

'Ow!' cried Elephant.

'Eee!' cried Elephant.

'Ah!' cried Elephant.
'I nearly got stuck.'

'You are funny,' cried Monkey, doubling up laughing, and not trying to help Elephant, *at all*.

Monkey switched on the radio. The music was very loud.

'Let's dance!' cried Monkey.

'Is that what friends do?' asked Elephant.

'Of course!' cried Monkey. 'Come on.'

'Ow!' cried Elephant.

'Eee!' cried Elephant.

'Ah!' cried Elephant.
'I can't dance.'

'You are funny,' cried Monkey, spinning round on
one leg, and not trying to help Elephant, *at all*.

'We'll have scrambled eggs on toast for supper,' said Monkey.

'I don't like scrambled eggs on toast,' said Elephant.

'I do!' cried Monkey. 'I'll let you be cook and we'll eat supper together.'

'Is that what friends do?' asked Elephant.

'Of course!' cried Monkey.

'Ah!' cried Elephant.

'Eee!' cried Elephant.

'Ow!' cried Elephant.
'I can't cook.'

'You are funny!' laughed Monkey, sitting up at
the table, and not trying to help Elephant, *at all.*

'Bedtime,' announced Monkey. 'Stay the night and you can sleep in my chair.'

'Is that what friends do?' asked Elephant, trying to make himself comfortable.

'Of course,' yawned Monkey.

'Ow!' cried Elephant.

'Eee!' cried Elephant.

'Ah!' cried Elephant. 'I'm falling off.'

Monkey didn't even stir.
He slept very well. He
snored very loudly.

Elephant didn't sleep one wink. Not even with cotton wool stuffed into his ears.

Next morning, Monkey woke up early.

'Come on, Elephant,' he cried. 'Let's go climbing.'

'I don't like climbing, especially before breakfast,' said Elephant.

'I do,' cried Monkey. 'We can climb together.'

'Is that what friends do?' asked Elephant.

'Of course!' cried Monkey, putting on his jacket.

Elephant shivered outside the door.

'Hurry up, Elephant!' called Monkey.
'We can climb this tree.'

'Is that what friends do?' asked Elephant.

'Of course!' cried Monkey, already
shinning high into the branches.

Elephant started to climb.
Crack went the branch.
Crash went Elephant.
'**Ahhhhhhhhhhhh!**'
cried Elephant.

'Eee!' cried Elephant.

'Ow!' cried Elephant.

'I can't climb.'

Monkey slid down the tree.
   'Ah,' said Monkey.
   'Eee,' said Monkey.
   'Oh dear,' said Monkey, looking into a big hole,
and not being able to see Elephant, *at all*.

Monkey was all alone.

Further along the bank Elephant sat gloomily. All alone.
Monkey came walking by.
'Oh, there you are, Elephant,' cried Monkey.
'Go away!' growled Elephant.

Monkey was very quiet. 'Elephant,' he said,
'you know I said I'd had lots of friends?'
　　'Yes,' sighed Elephant.
　　'Well,' said Monkey, 'none of them stayed
friends for long.'

Elephant was quiet. Monkey was quiet. They were thinking.

'Elephant,' said Monkey, after a while, 'perhaps I got it all wrong.'

'Oh?' said Elephant.

'Elephant,' said Monkey. 'Perhaps friends are kind to each other and share things.'

'Oh!' said Elephant.

'Elephant,' said Monkey. 'Shall we try again?'
'Is that what friends do?' asked Elephant.

'Of course!' cried Monkey.
And they gave each other a great, big hug.

More Red Fox picture books
for you to enjoy

MUMMY LAID AN EGG
by Babette Cole

RUNAWAY TRAIN
by Benedict Blathwayt

DOGGER
by Shirley Hughes

WHERE THE WILD THINGS ARE
by Maurice Sendak

OLD BEAR
by Jane Hissey

MISTER MAGNOLIA
by Quentin Blake

ALFIE GETS IN FIRST
by Shirley Hughes

OI! GET OFF OUR TRAIN
by John Burningham

GORGEOUS
by Caroline Castle and Sam Childs